January Stones 2013

January Stones 2013

by Gill James

Chapeltown Books

British Library Cataloguing in Publication Data

A Record of this Publication is available from the British Library

ISBN 978-1-910542-10-1

This edition published 2017 by Chapeltown Books
Manchester, England

All Chapeltown books are published on paper derived from sustainable
resources.

CONTENTS

INTRODUCTION

These stories were written one a day throughout January 2013. They were originally published on a blog called *Gill's January Stones*. In fact, they were published in reverse order. The first one you read here, *When Physics Got Sick*, was the last one to be written and originally published on 31 January 2016.

Sometimes the stories would come right at the beginning of the day. Sometimes they would take a while longer.

Do they have a theme? Not really, though the idea of 'stones' is one of turning them over slowly on the beach until we find the right one. It's not a bad time of year, anyway, right at the beginning in January, as the New Year starts and the days slowly become longer.

There was no strict word count. Each story is as long as it needs to be.

In any case, each one stayed with me until it felt finished. It had to be finished though, by midnight of that day.

As I've put this volume together, I've edited them again. This just goes to show how we've never actually finished editing.

Quite possibly if I ever perform any of these pieces for you, I'll edit them again before I read them out loud.

Gill James
January 2017

WHEN PHYSICS GOT SICK

The Scientist carefully took the shards of glass out of the cupboard, dropped them in the sink, and watched underwhelmed as the tumbler formed itself. It seemed natural, as if it had happened a thousand times before. Yet his constantly questioning mind wondered whether this, this first occurrence of something quite extraordinary, marked the beginning of the end as the second law of thermodynamics was breaking down.

As he filled the tumbler with water he became aware that at the same time as being in his kitchen he was also upstairs and at the other side of the universe, so clearly Planck's Constant had suddenly become somewhat bigger.

Later, examining the internal structure of protons, he found that they were indeed made of cream cheese and constantly mumbled nonsensical German so the label "quark" was actually extremely apt. Yet there was a paradox because surely the cream cheese itself was made of atoms, and they, in turn, of protons.

And yet.

There was no problem for Newton. Apples still fell merrily on the heads of those foolish enough to sit under apple-trees in the autumn. The big nuclear reactor in the sky still reacted. His home planet appeared to be carrying on its Maypole dance around its star and keeping up its complex ceilidh with the rest of the universe.

The Scientist paused for a moment and pondered. Perhaps the Humanities people were right after all. Every physicist knew that all of these laws did not work all of the time. Everything was relative anyway – Einstein had shown this. There could be a god, then. Or maybe the Matrix was not so far-fetched. It might even be the philosophers who had got it right – that life is but an illusion.

~~~~~~~~~

Scientific advice by Doctor Martin James who identified two subatomic particles, some ten years or so before the World Wide Web was born at CERN, thereby gobsmacking his children's science teachers.

WEATHER BEHAVING BADLY

They talked about El Niño and La Niña. So we had quite a few years of proper summer unfortunately accompanied by drought. Then we had several years of miserable weather. They talked of Global Warming and then renamed it Climate Change because the Warming was actually making it cooler for the posh people. But we hadn't seen anything yet.

They made a film about a new ice age arriving suddenly. It seemed melodramatic. Then came Katrina and the film seemed more reasonable. After Sandy it began to look tame.

The stream winds started moving in the wrong direction. We got snow on snow followed by rain on rain and floods, followed by temperatures going up overnight. Two feet of snow fell and disappeared within twenty-four hours.

Yet, one morning soon after, there was thick ice on the windscreen and cars sliding round the S bend though the temperature gauge said it was six degrees Celsius. Later, after the sun had shone all day and the gauge now said seven, there was, once more, ice on the car.

What's going on?

WHEN TIME WENT CRAZY

The Jenkins were not the sort of people to party all night, right through to breakfast. In their youth maybe, but not these days. Nevertheless, there they were, eating brunch and wondering where the night had gone.

"Did we finish the wine last night?"

"I don't think so. We didn't play Scrabble either."

It was a real puzzle. The last either could remember before they started breakfast was that they hadn't quite finished their dessert from the evening before.

Something must have happened, though, because they were wearing different clothes now.

"It's really funny," he said. "That lemon sorbet was making me quite full but I'm starving now. What's going on?"

"It's weird about the photos as well," she replied.

They carried on looking at the shots of Gibraltar on his phone. They weren't due to go there until the next day.

As the plane landed he shook his head. "I was looking forward to my beach day on Sunday. Now I've got to go to work tomorrow."

A short while later they were lying on the sun beds at the beach.

"I think I must be dreaming," he said.

"Well, so am I then. But don't you think it's funny that we're both having the same dream?"

"Hmm."

"Anyway, don't forget the photos." She picked up his iPhone and started searching. "Oh my. It looks as if our Sandra will marry Tony after all."

She handed him the phone. There was their daughter in a flowing white dress and Tony smarter than they'd ever seen him before. Judging by the colour of the leaves on the trees it was already autumn, but was that this year or another one?

POLITE SOCIETY

Rod wound down the window.

"Good morning sir."

"Good morning, officer."

"I presume you know that you are driving without insurance?"

Was he? The heck he was. He paid for it monthly on a direct debit. What was he on about?

"I pay for it every month."

"Well, perhaps there wasn't enough in your bank account, sir."

Could that be it? It might be. Every month he would get letters from the bank telling him he'd spent money he hadn't got and charging him £8.00 for the privilege.

"Could I see your driving license, sir?"

"I don't have it with me."

"Well you'll need to report to your nearest police station with it within ten days. Plus proof of insurance."

"I understand."

"Of course, I can't let you drive the car away. I suggest you give your insurance company a quick call."

Rod found the details out of the glove box. The police car's Stop sign mocked him as he waited for someone at the call centre to pick up. He only had to wait four minutes but it seemed a lot longer as the cars whizzed by on the motorway.

"That's right," said the girl at the other end after he'd explained the situation. "Your last payment didn't go through, even though we tried it twice. Could you make a payment now?"

He managed to find a card that still had some credit on it. The next two minutes passed even more slowly than the previous four.

"That's all gone through. We've sent a text message to confirm. The police database is updated instantly."

The police man tapped the window again. "That's all in order now, sir. We'll let you off with a caution this time. You'll still have to make that little trip to your local station, though. Just remember to keep an eye on your bank account in future. Rightio, I'll help you get back on to the motorway. Have a good day now."

Rod wound his window back up and gave the officer the thumbs up sign.

As he merged into the traffic he wondered why he'd been so damned polite. He wasn't a criminal. He hadn't deliberately avoided paying his insurance. He was just too busy earning not quite enough money to find the time to check what the bank was doing with it.

ABIGAIL'S SNOWMAN

It was all going to melt soon. By this time tomorrow it would all be gone. It was so completely freakish. Almost a foot of snow in the early hours and throughout the morning, and now mid-afternoon, cars were driving reasonably easily through deep slush. Yet, if you wanted to get the car off the drive, you needed to clear the pavement.

She'd done that. And now she had an interesting pile of snow. "We should make it into a snowman," she'd said to Jeff and Lester.

"Mum, I'm a bit past that, don't you think?"

"I suppose." She remembered when Lester had been a little boy and had got so excited about the snow. Now he was just miffed that he couldn't go off on his mountain-bike.

"It's not worth the effort. It'll all be gone in a matter of hours." Jeff shook his head.

"Well, I'm going to do it."

She'd actually enjoyed shovelling the snow into a big heap. It had been better than being cooped up inside and the exercise not only kept her warm but also made her feel good. She didn't want to stop.

She formed and honed the lump of snow into something vaguely human-shaped. She straightened his side, moulded arms and a square head with ears on it. She plumped his cheeks, shaped hands, and then fingers. She added, subtracted and sculpted.

Soon two pairs of eyes were looking at her through the window. The front door opened. "I've found these round the back," said Jeff. "I thought they might do for his eyes, nose and mouth." He handed her some of the dark pebbles off the Japanese garden.

Lester appeared at his side. "I know what else." He dashed inside. He came back with the matching plaid scarf and ear-muffs Great Aunt Tilda had given him last Christmas.

"And I know what we need now." Abigail was adding the finishing touches as the two men in her life looked on. "Go and get my sunglasses. The big round ones."

Jeff came back with them. She placed them carefully on the snowman's face. "Perfect," she said.

"Not bad," said Jeff.

Lester took pictures on his iPhone.

When Abigail woke up in the night and looked through the spare bedroom window to see how well the snow was thawing, her snowman was decidedly slimmer. By then next morning his head had rolled off and the scarf, muffs and sunglasses were lying on the ground. By the following afternoon he was just a lump of snow that was barely recognisable as something someone had made.

"It doesn't matter," Abigail whispered. "You were still worth it." Tomorrow would come soon enough and she would have to be all po-faced and straight-laced at the station. Even a copper deserved a bit of fun now and again.

GLADLY

He was absolutely unbelievable, Kerry decided. He must have been in his sixties easily. Him and his wife. And what a get up. Hiking boots, bright yellow socks, knee-length trousers, tweed jacket, woolly red bobble hat, one of those long walking sticks and a serious hiker's rucksack. Just a small one.

His wife was no more elegant. She was short and rather stubby. The bright red duffle coat, blue trousers and pink wellies did not help. And of course, she had a red bobble hat to match her husband's. She'd probably knitted both of them.

Fancy going out walking in this weather. True, the snow had stopped but everywhere was either icy and slippery or wet and muddy, depending on where the sun had been shining. He'd obviously fallen over. He had mud all the way up his side. Both of them had really red cheeks. With those and the hats they looked just as if they'd come straight from Lapland and helping Santa.

And what was this they were now putting on the conveyor belt? Fresh pasta. Cook-in sauce. A bottle of the finest single-malt whisky the store sold. The little wife grinned almost shyly at him and he winked.

It was all right for some. She would be stuck here for another three hours. Same old routine. Ring 'em up. Bag 'em up. Take the money or process the card. Yawn, yawn.

Her till was just opposite the in-store café. She was enjoying a slight lull between customers when something made her look over there. The red hats! She'd know them anywhere. The bottle of whisky was sticking up out of his rucksack. He was carrying a tray on which were a frothy, cream-topped hot chocolate, a banana milkshake, a doughnut and a slice of cheese cake and the little wife was pointing eagerly at a table near the window. Yep. Definitely all right for some.

He spotted her looking at him. He grinned. "Cheer up, lass. Everybody has to make their own gladness."

He had a point, she supposed.

Her next customer arrived. "Are you all right there?" she said, offering her brightest smile.

MY SISTER'S WEDDING

It went amazingly, actually. I never thought it would. I mean, bad enough that she was marrying Drippy Kevin. It didn't start well either. The car carrying her and my dad broke down on the way. Kevin mucked the words up. Just like you'd expect, actually. No surprises there. And it started raining just as they started taking the photos.

The worse, though, was when they run out of wine at the reception. Nobody could work out why. It wasn't as if anybody was putting it away unnecessarily. And Dad swears to God he ordered enough. He worked it out very carefully with the manager at the Red Lion.

Chris came to the rescue. He's the son of my dad's best mate Joe. Joe's a cabinet-maker and my dad's a fitter. They were at college together. Chris is his oldest son. He was always like a big brother to me. Following in his dad's footsteps, he is now. Makes all sorts of interesting furniture. Not married either, though he'd be a good catch.

Anyway, he saved the day. "Bring out lots of jugs of water," he said.

"You can't let them drink water," I said.

"Trust me, they won't know the difference."

It's funny. We didn't. In fact, the water tasted just like wine. As it ran out, the hotel staff just brought out more water. It even looked like wine in the glasses – you know, slightly yellow and not quite clear. And as we toasted the bride and groom, everybody seemed to have bubbles in their glasses.

Nobody got drunk, but everybody grew mellow. People who had not been speaking to each other for years started talking again. Our family got to know Kevin's family. Even Drippy Kevin seemed less drippy by the end.

I don't know what that Chris did. Perhaps it was some sort of magic. Or perhaps he hypnotised us all. I suppose he might have nipped round to the Cash and Carry while nobody was looking. Whatever. It's a waste, him being a cabinet-maker.

Funny thing though. What my uncle said to my dad when everybody was leaving.

"Good do, that, little bro'. Unusual, though, serving the better wine last."

THE NEW RED COAT

"Lady in Red," croaked a familiar and unwanted voice.

It would be. Andy Wolf. Why did he have to be here? Spoiling everything. It had all been going beautifully to plan. She was wrapped up warm in her new red duffle coat with the retro toggles and the lovely warm fake-fur-lined hood. She and Tom were going for a walk in the snow and then they were going to have a pub meal. Now she'd got to get rid of this pest first.

"You been round your grandma's recently? You should go an' check up on her."

What? Had he been harassing her grandma again? Andy Wolf's gang was notorious for playing tricks on the old folk on the estate. She'd better go and check. She took out her mobile to ring Tom to warn him she'd be late only to find that the battery was dead.

Darn! She'd better be quick.

Twenty minutes later she arrived at her grandma's house. She found the key under the flower pot but was surprised to see that the door was already open. She'd have to tell her about that. It could be dangerous, especially with people like Andy Wolf around.

But she needn't have worried. There was Grandma, safe and sound, wrapped up in layers of blankets. She felt a weight lift from her chest.

"Oh, Grandma, you can put the heating on you know. And you

shouldn't leave the door unlocked."

Grandma turned and growled at her. Only it wasn't Grandma. It was Andy Wolf. He must have got there on his motorbike. He roared and sprang up at her.

"What have you done with my grandma?"

"Oh not a lot compared with what I'm going to do with you." He grabbed her arm.

She screamed.

The front door suddenly burst open.

Not more of them, she thought. She was sure she was going to pass out.

"Put her down," shouted another familiar but this time welcome voice.

Tom! But how did he know where she was?

Andy ran for the front door. It was useful having a boyfriend who was policeman. The local wild boys respected him even when he wasn't on duty.

"What's going on down here?" Grandma shuffled down the stairs. So Andy hadn't hurt her thank goodness. Her face cracked into a wide grin when she noticed Tom. "Oh I see you've brought your young man again."

"What do you say?" whispered Tom. "We come and live here with your grandma when you become Mrs Forrester?"

Her cheeks burned. She was sure they must match her coat. Did he really mean what he thought he meant?

"Well, will you?" His eyes twinkled.

Grandma looked bemused. She probably couldn't hear what they were saying. Just as well really.

"Of course," she whispered. "But how did you know I'd come here?"

"You said you'd got a new red coat. You can see it a mile off. I just followed you. Practising my detectives skills, see. I'm after promotion."

"I don't know what you two are on about but I'm going to put the kettle on. I like your new coat, by the way. Very smart. That'll keep the wolves away."

THE BOATMAN

He brushed on the last of the sealant. There. She would keep the water out all right now. He could move her to a safer spot once the waters came. There was enough petrol for several days journey and then there were sails. In any circumstances she would float beautifully.

His wife appeared with a basket full of bread, cheese and fruit. "You're still bent on doing this?"

He nodded.

"They'll take you for a fool." She scurried away, shaking her head.

Two lads from the village strolled by.

"Hey, mister, who do you think you am? Noah?"

"What you going to put on there? Copulating kangaroos?" They started pelting him and the boat with pebbles.

He didn't say anything but carried on eating his lunch.

He looked at the sky. It was getting blacker. *Any time now,* he thought. *I don't blame you for breaking your promise. We're worse than ever.*

The first drops of rain started. Time to load up. The dairy herd first. Then the bullocks and the sheep. He hoped the kids would cope with the chickens and the working dogs. And he must make sure to get them and the missus aboard.

No, he wasn't going to lose his farm for anything. Mother Nature, Global Warming, Climate change or the anger of the one true god. Not with that boat he wasn't. Then who would be laughing?

BEAUTY SLEEPING

"I told you," said Rosie's Aunty Pat. "I told you she would turn out like this. "You could tell as soon as she was born. I warned you at her christening."

"You weren't even invited," mumbled Mrs Red, Rosie's mum. "And you almost ruined it." She cleared her throat. "I'm just glad we found her in time."

"She'll die, I tell you."

"Please don't say that." Mrs Red began dabbing at her eyes.

"Ladies," said the young doctor. "I'll have to ask you to wait outside. My patient needs her rest."

Jude went to ask if he could stay but the words stuck like thorns in his throat. The doctor seemed to understand. He put a hand on Jude's shoulder. "You stay with her, Mr Prince. Talk to her. It might help her. It will certainly help you. We'll know more once we've completed the tox screen."

Jude took her hand. "You're beautiful," he whispered. "I just wish you'd wake up."

He talked to her, telling her all sorts of nonsense, stroked her arm, held her hand and kissed her fingers. She didn't wake up though.

Nurse Good came into the room. "Mr Prince, I have news," she said. "It's not an overdose. She's an insulin-dependent diabetic. Didn't you know?"

Jude shook his head.

"You know that might be why she left home in the first place. People sometimes like to keep this to themselves." She placed her hand on Jude's arm. "Don't be too hard on her, but now that you know you can help her. She's not going to die. We can soon get her sugar level up. Keep talking and let her know you'll be there when she wakes up."

It was chaotic for a few minutes as the doctor gave commands and Nurse Good and another nurse added things to her drip.

"She's not quite out of the woods yet," said the doctor. "But she stands more chance if you stay with her."

Then it was just him and her. He would get her out of those woods. He felt as if he was chopping down undergrowth to get through to her. He carried on talking, cajoling, explaining, telling jokes and just staring at her when he ran out of things to say.

A shaft of sunlight came through the window suddenly and lit up her face.

"You're so beautiful," he whispered. He couldn't help it. He just leant forward and kissed her on the lips.

Her eyelids fluttered a little and then she opened her eyes fully. "Oh, my Mr Prince, it's you."

A little colour returned to her cheeks. She giggled.

She was going to be all right. Jude leant forward and kissed her again.

PEAK FITNESS

The remains of lunch and three half-eaten birthday cakes are packed away.

"Decision time," says our leader. "This is where we part. Those who want to go the short way take this path. If you want to do the full eight miles – follow me. We've already done two and a half, by the way."

I hesitate. My legs and feet are hardy. My lungs less so. But really, five and a half miles is not much for me.

"There's only short steep bit." She seems to read my mind.

We wave to the others and start up a piece of open peak, into a bitter wind and light but penetrating drizzle. No one says a word. We are all thinking that maybe we shouldn't have attempted this.

Two weeks ago, still mid-April it had been warm and pleasant here. Now, the day before the May bank holiday it is cold and damp. Even more so than in Rainy City. We are high up here.

We turn around the peak. We are no longer going up and the wind is behind us. The rain stops. We become almost warm. We take it in turns to lead and there are moments of doubt but we trust our collective consciousness. We don't worry. Oddly, though it is grey and there is no sun my reactive lenses go dark.

We reach the part where we have to climb. I'm the last to arrive at the top and breathing hurts. But folk are patient and they don't actually have to wait long. Besides, others complain of a struggle. Then we're on the home straight and I'm actually in the lead more often than not.

We join the short-walkers at the café in the park and drink cups of tea. We finish off the cake. Gradually we drift apart and make our way back to cars and the train station. But not before friends of friends have become close friends.

The next day I'm barely stiff and my feet don't hurt. Several others are complaining. Do I have Peak fitness?

MONDAYS

Trevor sat in the conservatory, drinking the last of the Sunday dinner wine.

"Are you coming through?" Marion called.

"Just doing my list," he replied.

Trevor wasn't a man to dread Mondays. "Waste of energy," he always said. "Worrying your life away."

Even so, he always liked to put his list together. It wasn't a "to do" list, really. It was more a "what's the worst that can happen" list.

He started tapping into his phone.

Wilkins will be horrified when he knows that the Granada project has gone to Building and Planning.

Wilkins will be difficult anyway – he'll take a while to get going after six months sick leave.

The beta trial starts tomorrow. It could go pear-shaped and we'll have to start again.

Smith and Anderson haven't contacted me. I bet there'll have been some panic emails over the weekend.

Email anyway.

That would **do.** That was all enough to worry about. He refused to start looking at emails at the weekend. But it always meant there were a lot on a Monday morning.

"Is it done?" Marion had popped her head through the conservatory door.

"Yep. I think so." He downed the very last of the wine. He held up his glass. "Shall we open another?"

She shrugged. "I wish you wouldn't get so het up about Mondays," she said.

"I don't really." He looked at his list again. Looking at it, working out what to expect somehow made it easier. And with this lot to contend with at least the week would pass quickly and he'd soon be relaxing at home again. "Just making sure I know what's what so I can enjoy the rest of my Sunday."

Marion rolled her eyes. "Go on then. I'll get another bottle."

"Good show."

A JOURNEY IN THE SNOW

The concert ends later than I'd thought it would. In fact, I should have been back half an hour ago and it's at least an hour's drive from here. I phone home.

"Really?" he says. "It's snowing quite heavily here."

Oh.

There are a few flakes tumbling as we go to our cars. I have to smile as a fellow choir member and her passengers fail to find theirs.

It is warm and cosy as I set off. My head still buzzes from the joy of the concert. Though we were cold the atmosphere was glorious. The music on Classic FM is exquisite. The snowflakes are large and turn to water as they hit the ground. We'll be all right.

But as we join the ring road and head north it becomes more serious. The snow is sticking and crunches under our wheels. We form a convoy – two or three small cars and a couple of lorries. It's good to have professional drivers on board.

I remind myself. "Drive positively. If you skid, drive into it."

We negotiate crossing four lanes at an interchange that is tricky at the best of times. But where I should cross another two lanes and come off I chicken out. I cannot see the road at all and know that there is a raised pavement in the middle. I stay with the convoy and go into town, getting off at the next exit.

I just need to go up the ramp, across the top and down the other side.

As I turn off the slip road I skid a little and it's almost fun – like ice-skating in a car. There's nothing to hit. I remember my own earlier advice. A split second later the car is straight again. My heart rate's up, though. Lurking at the back of my mind is the memory of writing off a similar car in similar conditions. Still, this car is more stable: it has power steering and front-wheel drive. The other was manual, rear-wheel and had all the weight at the back.

I'm on my own going back but it's not too bad. And once I'm off the express way I can walk the rest if need be. It's only a couple of miles.

I turn into the road that leads into the village next to where we live. There's a bit of a steep hill but now it's only one and a half miles. It's stopped snowing. A walk in the snow might actually be quite pleasant.

A car swings out of the pub car-park and I have to slow down. Curses. It slows me even more as I have to wait for it to turn right. Will I have enough momentum to get up the hill? Still, only one mile now.

The car chugs along, easily climbing, though I sense the ice underneath. But we make it to the top.

The next challenge will be the S-bend and the parked cars on our untreated road. I take it steady. I keep the revs high, like they tell you to. And finally, I'm home.

I turn on to the drive. But it won't have it. The car slides and slips and threatens to bash the one next to it. I don't want to leave it on the street.

Another car might bump into it.

I hammer on the door. "We've got to clear the drive," I cry when he comes out.

It takes less than ten minutes and I park the car safely.

I enjoy a stiff drink. It's now well after midnight: the journey that should have lasted an hour has taken two and a half. My heart is still thumping. But actually, though I wouldn't choose to do that drive if I didn't have to, I have quite enjoyed the challenge.

HOUSING ADDICT

The couple on the lifestyle TV programme admired the lounge. "The only trouble is," said the woman, "I don't like the beams."

The presenter tried to hide a splutter.

The beams are the whole point, thought Kath. *That's why you move to the country.*

What would a Christmas tree look like in the lounge? Good, she thought.

The people on the television moved into the kitchen. Hmm. It had a range but no other means of cooking. Would they ever learn how to operate a monster like that? Did you have to have it on in summer and did it make the kitchen too hot? The kitchen was otherwise superb – plenty of cupboards, plenty of surfaces, an island and plenty of room for a table. There was a separate dining room too. Upstairs the two studies and spare bedroom she and Rob would need.

"It's all a bit small," said the woman on the television.

"Let's go outside," said the presenter.

The gardens were really pretty. Kath could see herself out there in the summer.

"Maybe there's not quite enough land," said the woman.

The woman and her husband didn't agree on anything. The second house had the sea view they wanted but was too isolated. The third house had all the land but it sloped too much. The mystery house was a converted chapel. Kath loved the idea of chapel and barn conversions but this one left her cold. She couldn't see Christmas with the family there. She couldn't see lazy summer days outdoors.

No, her favourite was the very first one. The TV couple agreed in the end. They put in an offer that was accepted and they are due to move there soon. They are going to put in false ceilings to hide the beams. Madness.

Kath sighed. There was no way she could afford the amount they were going to pay. But what did she want really? If, say, she won the lottery?

Quaint or modern?

Seaside or country?

In the village or out in the wilds?

Home or abroad?

Huge, just big enough or warm and cosy?

No, she really couldn't decide. No wonder the universe wouldn't give her what she wanted – she didn't know what that was.

It was getting dark. She drew the curtains and gave the pretty suburban street a last look. At least she couldn't see another house exactly the same as theirs. The gardens were neat, the neighbours were quiet and through the upstairs window, if you looked between the houses opposite, you could see the snow-covered hills in the distance. There were some nice walks round here yet they were quite near to a major city.

Yes, the lounge was just big enough – there was room for the grand piano and it was easy to keep warm even on the coldest days. They each had a study. They could eat in the kitchen but had a more formal dining area as well. Maybe, then, she already had it. The ideal house.

She sighed again. What a bore. All the fun came in looking.

ART EXAM

It was different from other exams she'd had to invigilate. The students weren't sitting in rows at little desks. They were in semi-circle, tucked behind their easels. There was the normal exquisite silence however. But not the apprehension. She could tell by their faces that they were engaged and committed, ready to show off their best. They worked away with their pencils, brushes and charcoal sticks, never getting eye-contact with her or with each other.

Sun streamed through the large window, colouring the parquet floor toffee. Particles of dust floated in the light. She could see snowdrops outside and the crocuses looked ready to burst into flower. Even the daffodils had stems.

Still no sound except that of the pencils, brushes and charcoal sticks on the paper and occasionally of swirled water. She was warm and calm. It was so much easier to be here than in a class of fourteen-year-olds trying to distract her. Nobody could touch her here. Nobody could make any demands.

The students were working on a still-life. A tray of cheeses, a crusty loaf and a glass of celery sticks had been tastefully arranged on a table covered with a cream cloth. Each student saw it differently, she realised as she walked behind them and as unobtrusively as possible looked at each one's work. It was not just because they were looking from slightly different angles. Stylised celery, here, almost a photograph there and one or two seeming to have no connection at all with what was on the table.

Someone should have come to relieve her by now, but she didn't care; she was enjoying being inside this bubble. But she was hungry as there'd been no time for breakfast. She'd overslept a little because she'd been marking her own exam papers until 4.00 a.m. that morning.

Her tummy rumbled. She reached over and took one of the celery sticks.

The silence was shattered as she bit into it.

Then it returned, now more intense, as all activity stopped and twelve pairs of eyes now at last looked into hers.

THE WELL-TRAVELLED CAMEMBERT

The kids made their way off the bus, clutching their souvenirs from a day trip to France.

"Make sure you've got everything," called their teacher.

After they'd all gone, she and her colleagues inspected the seats and overhead luggage rack. "You always get one, don't you?" she said, holding up a decent size Camembert. "I'll take this home and bring it back on Monday."

"You're not putting that stinky thing in our fridge," said her husband.

She left it in the garage.

By the time she arrived at school on Monday the cheese was getting rather ripe. She decided it would be better to leave it under her car rather than in it.

As soon as she got in she composed an announcement for the daily bulletin.

If anyone left a Camembert, i.e. a French cheese, on the bus on Friday, it is now under my car, the blue Beetle, on the west car park. Please help yourself.

Not everyone listens to the bulletin and one student who had a cold and who was shortly going to a music festival certainly hadn't. He spotted the cheese under the car. He and his mate went over to inspect it further.

"Looks like somebody's lost their cheese," he said. "I'll take it to lost property."

"No time," said his mate. "The bus is here, look."

The cheese was stuffed into a bag, taken to the music festival, and then left in a heated bedroom overnight.

"What's that horrible smell?" the boy's mother asked in the morning. "Have you been forgetting to put your dirty washing away again?"

The boy remembered the cheese. "It's all right, Mum. I'll deal with it."

As soon as he arrived at school he took the cheese straight to lost property. "It's a bit whiffy," said the school secretary. "I'll put it in the newsletter. But if nobody collects it today, it'll have to go."

The French exchange group arrived that evening. No doubt some of the students brought less adventurous Camembert for their hosts. The teachers met later in the week at the home of the couple who were putting up the organisers. The hosts were providing a main course and others were bringing wine, cheese, appetizers, chocolates and dessert.

"Excellent meal," said the Head of Department as they all sat finishing off their wine and cheese.

"Indeed," said one of the French teachers. "And I've never tasted such an exquisite Camembert."

"Ah, well, there's a story about that," said the colleague who had brought it.

Which just goes to show; Camembert improves with travelling.

SAVING A HERD

She looked at the body of the old matriarch. She was certainly dead. The younger female knew there was something wrong with the food here and hungry as she and the others were, they shouldn't eat it. It had killed their leader.

The matriarch's calf nudged its mother, urging her to her feet. He wanted to feed. The younger female knew she had enough milk for him as well as her own little calf, who was a couple of months younger. How could she convince him to take her milk, though?

She rubbed her trunk along the corps and then waved it along her body. That might not be enough, though. She scrambled on to the body of her former leader and rubbed her full udder along it. Some milk spilled from her swollen teats and both her own calf and the one whose mother had died galloped towards her. It seemed to be working then.

But another female and a young male mistook her intent and charged towards her, bellowing furiously. She trotted away, the two calves following her swiftly. As soon as she was out of the way the other two left her alone and she was able to feed the two calves in peace. She noticed, though, that the two who had threatened her drifted over towards the food that the matriarch had been eating. The others began to follow. She knew they mustn't do that. There was something wrong with that food.

She pulled herself away from the two calves and galloped over to where

41

the others were beginning to feed. It was her turn to bellow now. The young male charged her, followed by the female who was nearly as big as her. Something snapped inside her. They must not eat that food. They just must not. She lashed out with her trunk. She clapped the female around the head, sending her swirling in a drunken dance. She bashed the male's left foreleg just below the knee. He toppled to the ground.

She bellowed once more and then moved towards where she thought the food would safe. The calves, although disappointed at having their feed interrupted, were actually full. They followed meekly. One by one the rest of the herd joined them.

The next priority was to get the calves covered in mud. Both of them were a little strange. They had pink eyes and white skin. The white skin burned easily and made them a good target for the hunters. Yet once they were covered in mud they looked like any other elephant. She led them down to the river and started squirting the cool sticky mud over them and encouraging them to do the same. Gradually the rest of the herd followed. Soon they were all in the water and many of them were helping to rub the mud into the little white calves' skin.

The babies were safe now. Hidden from the hunters and protected from the sun. They now must find a bigger supply of safe food. They must move away from here. Hopefully they would find something before it got too dark.

She led them out of the water. Her own calf hooked his trunk round her tail and the older one hooked himself to his. Two calf-less females flanked the outside. Other family groups walked behind, all linked together. Younger males brought up the rear. It dawned on her slowly that she was the new matriarch and was leading them to their new life.

MOULES MARINIÈRE

She didn't like this time of year. It was still dark and cold. Christmas had gone. At least in December you had all of that to look forward to.

She wasn't even sure she wanted to prepare this particular dish. But it was the next thing on the list and she was a woman of lists. And there would be three quarters of a bottle of wine left for later.

The last time they'd had mussels they'd been the big fat ones from a different continent. They'd been ugly and rubbery and a bit too – well – mussel. She actually preferred the smaller, sweeter European ones – the ones they pickled and served with chips.

These were the smaller ones in fact, though the pint weighed heavy, she realised as she scrubbed off barnacles, pulled off beards and discarded just two that had already opened.

Next she chopped onions. The recipe actually said shallots but at least the onions were shallot shaped. She supplemented them with spring onions and garlic. The butter melted in the cast-iron pan and soon the vegetables were softening in the sizzling yellow liquid. Next in went the mussels. Already the shells began to open, exposing soft pinky orange flesh.

In went the wine – a quarter of bottle – a good amount of freshly chopped parsley and a small bay leaf. On went the lid, and few minutes later, once the lid was too hot to touch, down went the heat. The part-baked baguette warmed in the oven.

The kitchen filled with the pleasantest of cooking smells.

A few moments later it was ready.

With the first mouthful the winter gloom lifted. "This combination of tastes is so right," she said.

"You wonder how they found out, don't you? This couldn't have happened by accident."

One mouthful at a time winter despair was banished. A watery sun even peeped out between the grey clouds. This dish should certainly stay on the list.

THE IT EXPERT

She really didn't know how she – or anyone else for that matter – could do without him. He could get a virus out of a machine in seconds. He could make programmes that other people had set up work better. He even knew how the machines worked physically. Amazingly, although his hands were quite big, he could still get inside the computers and tinker with their hardware.

"Does anybody else know all this stuff?" she asked him.

"Just me and a few more."

"So what'll happen when you die? Will all that knowledge be lost? Will it all die with you?"

He shrugged. "Won't be a problem. I'm going to live forever."

She didn't believe him.

She didn't even pick up the clue when, not realising that she was watching, he took the lasagne out of the oven without using oven gloves. She knew as well that he could put his finger in a power socket and suffer no ill effects. She couldn't explain any of this and didn't really try. He'd always been peculiar. But that very strangeness made him so much of an IT expert.

Then she found him one morning, lying at the foot of the stairs, his head crumpled. But no blood and grey matter were seeping out. Just wires and chips.

She contacted the people he worked for and they sent a guy round.

"Can you repair him?" she asked.

The man shook his head. "He was the only one who would have known how to."

"What about all of the other stuff?"

"Some of us know some of it."

"And if you fall down the stairs?"

The man shrugged and sucked his teeth.

After he'd left and taken the remains of the machine with him, she switched on her computer. She wondered who she would ask when she encountered a problem. How long would the internet carry on working? Would the planes soon start dropping out of the sky?

Droids are even more stupid than humans, she thought. She started searching for an IT support company.

12 JANUARY 2030: NO CRIME IN DEPTON

12 January 2030. Depton police reported that there had been no crimes in the last twenty-four hours.

"What on earth are we going to put on Chatterer?"

"Do you think we should get out some archive stuff? Keep them amused? We lose our Chatterer followers if we don't give them something to grumble about."

"Let alone what might happen to the advertising revenue. We'll run out of biscuits."

Later, when the Depton Ringer requested its daily upload of police stories an alarm prompted the webmaster to make a direct contact.

Is there a technical problem? You've not sent any crime reports.

We've had no crime.

So what can we put in the Ringer?

Some good news? Isn't "no crime" news?

The webmaster scratched his head. What the heck could he write? He reported on the lack of crime. He even visited the police archives and dug out a few stories and old pictures. Should he do a feature about how the local police kept themselves busy when there were no criminals to deal with?

Half way through the afternoon he was contacted by Depton Shopping City.

You call this news? If you can't produce anything better than this by the end of play today we're pulling the contract.

Straightaway the webmaster got on to the Chatterer clerk at Depton police station. "Can't you get something going? Don't you know some tame criminals who'll do a job or something? Liven the area up a bit."

"I'll see what I can do," she said. She looked at the biscuit tin. That was going to be a problem soon as well. "Serge," she called. "We've just had the Ringer on the communipad. He's complaining about lack of news. Wants us to set one up."

The sergeant scratched his head. "I guess Alfie Roberts owes us one. Get him on the communipad, will you? No, better use my personal one." He handed her his portable.

In the early hours of 13 January 2030 a disused warehouse was set on fire. It pointed to Alfie Roberts, known arsonist. However, the Depton police could find no proof and so could bring about no prosecution. The Depton Ringer attracted even more advertisers. The Depton police gathered even more followers on Chatterer and they earned more through advertising as well. They bought chocolate biscuits when the others ran out and offered Alfie one when he came in for a chat because he was bored.

EPIPHANY

"So, you see, it's distribution that's more of a problem. The mechanics of it needn't be, though. For about £8.50 a year – it varies according to how VAT varies – this particular Print On Demand provider will hook your title up to tons of distributers – people like Amazon as well. But it's still difficult getting the general public to notice the book. Still, you'll get a trickle of sales anyway, even if your marketing isn't all that dynamic. And you can set it up in such a way that it's impossible to lose money except maybe the set-up costs."

Alex enjoyed it actually when people asked him to talk about his publishing business. It reminded him that he actually loved producing books. Never mind the pitfalls – the titles that didn't sell, the authors who couldn't respond to editorial comment and the constant realisation that if he'd put as much effort into any other business as he had into this, he'd be making a heck of a lot more money.

She was a determined woman. Mid-fifties, he would have said. She'd made copious notes and asked him some really intelligent questions. Nothing he'd said seemed to shock her. She obviously already knew a fair bit about the publishing business.

Suddenly, though, she sat up straighter. Her eyes glazed over and she seemed to be looking at nothing in particular. Then she focussed and took up eye-contact with him again. "Look. I think I need to go now. Thank you so much. You've given me some really useful information." She stood up and started gathering her things.

"Well, don't hesitate to get in touch if I can be of any more help."

She nodded and scuttled away. Alex wondered whether she had a bus to catch or perhaps she was just trying to avoid the rush hour. It was ten past four.

He met her again a few months later. He'd been invited to what turned out to be a well-attended book launch. He spotted her in the crowd.

"So is this your imprint?" he said.

She shook her head. "It might have been though. Six of us were going to run it. Now it's just Colin and his wife." She nodded towards the table where the author was signing books and near to which the publisher and his lovely wife were talking enthusiastically to those waiting in the queue. "But my meeting with you was really helpful. It made me realise how much effort it all is. And it made me and the other three decide we'd rather put our energy into our writing. Leave all this to people like yourself who know what they're doing."

I do, do I? thought Alex.

The women, whose name he still didn't know, took another sip of her wine. She grinned. "Colin and Judy are publishing my book next month. Will you come to my launch as well?"

RIDING TRAMS

"We'll have to get a cab from Radcliffe. Shall we phone from Heaton Park or once we get there?"

"Unless we go right into Bury. Just to say that we've been to the end of every line."

"Oldham Mumps was a bit of a laugh, warn't it? I mean mumps. I always thought that was a disease men dreaded getting. Makes your private parts swell up and what not."

"Yeah. But Media City was something else. Never been there before. All that glass and fancy lighting. Hob-nobbing with the BBC. Salford's up itself in't it? Wonder what they think in Ordsall?"

"God knows. Then there's Eccles. Eccles. Eccles. If you keep on saying it, it don't half sound funny after a bit. Should have got some cakes while we was there."

"Well, are you going to open them chips or not? I'm bloody starving."

The intercom speaker crackled. "Put that food away or you'll have to get off at the next stop."

"Sorry, gov. We forgot." Bernie turned to Chris. "I guess that settles it then. Get off at Radcliffe and then phone. Then while we'm waiting we can finish our chips."

"Or we could walk into town and have another pint then get a cab."

"That sounds like a plan, my man. And we can eat the chips on the way to the pub. They're still hot and we're nearly in Prestwich."

"Yeah. You've got to celebrate when you get you free bus pass, haven't you? It only happens once in a lifetime."

"Except we can do it all again when Andy gets his."

SUMMER EVENING

The sun shines from the west, creating a patch of light on the sloping lawn. You can see the gnats dancing. They're nearly always there. Maybe there is an underground stream.

It is sticky and oppressive. Summers here are never blue sky and glorious. Today, there is only total inertia. No sounds and the thin hint of them muffled by a blanket of enforced siesta.

Then Jack next door barks. A door opens. There are children's voices and the sound of tea cups. A sprinkler swishes on. The air cools a little, just a little. An ice-cream plays *Greensleeves* at 100 miles an hour. Ice Dreams still has custom, it seems, despite the chest freezers in the garages.

A car pulls on to the drive, the engine stops and a door slams.

Afternoon is gone. I take the wine bottle out of the fridge and reach for two glasses. A summer evening has begun.

THE LANGUAGE EXPERT

Clive first came to languages by learning their grammar. Years later he told his own students: "You have to have grammar. Without grammar language is just a jelly that collapses without meaning." Yet seven years on, in real life, he couldn't even order a cheese sandwich in French.

His first students were subject to a sort of programing. It was a bit more than a drill but only just. It got them saying things. A few.

Then came Communicative Language Learning. "It doesn't matter how elegant the language is, the communication is the main thing." His students managed to get cheese sandwiches, fries and many other delights when they'd been learning for less than two years.

But it still wasn't enough for the advisors and inspectors. "It lacks fluency. It lacks accuracy. We need more Target Language."

Are we going back to the Direct Method? thought Clive. He remembered warning anecdotes from his tutor of the enthusiastic teacher of French who rushed into the classroom at the last minute every time crying "Bonjour, la classe." The class thought he was apologising for being late. But Clive also remembered his frequent visits to schools where foreign children learnt English and there was a sort of expectation that whole lessons would be conducted entirely in the "Target Language". Why wouldn't they be?

The Powers that Be thought languages should include creativity, but they couldn't work out what that really meant so they took it out of the curriculum again. Clive thought it was when one of his students sighed and said "Je déteste le professeur." He had just explained, very carefully, in the target language, what the objectives were for today's lesson. Or it might be when his students, just two weeks into their course, managed to write acrostic poems in German or before the end of the first year his students of Spanish managed to produce some fabulous haiku based on colour. And naturally, there was that young man who did brilliantly in his oral, even though he didn't deserve to, the lazy sod, because the night before he'd been chatting up the French girls, on exchange with a neighbouring school.

Then there was Computer Assisted Language Learning. That's started off crudely and got better when the language experts told the computer experts what they really, really wanted. And the Internet anyway, provided authentic experience and contact with native speakers, not to mention opportunities for tandem learning.

One day a very good German student of English said: "But we learnt the grammar very quickly. It's the best way to learn a language. It gives you the power to build it up." He thought she had a point and that what goes around comes around.

They were all right and they were all wrong, after all.

Motivation, he decided, was the key. Give them a reason to want to learn. They'll find their own way. Help them to make friends. That's what he did. He himself gained a lot of friends from different countries and helped others to do the same. He read and spoke fluently in three other languages, could manage a fourth and didn't get anywhere with a fifth. *Too old,* he concluded. *Palate's set. New dogs and old tricks etc.*

What he read taught him empathy and by the time he retired he didn't really know who he was anymore because he could understand so many points of view. Except, in the end, he decided, that after all, he quite liked a cosy afternoon in on a rainy day in the UK, with his books for company. Even if most of them weren't in English.

THE UNBELIEVER

Gladys Cooper did not believe the stories about the old TV presenter and his history of sexual abuse. Not even when her friend protested "But my mum's best friend was attacked by him and was too scared to say something back in the day."

"I think it's a load of people jumping on the bandwagon," another friend said.

Gladys agreed.

She did not believe there was anything peculiar about the geography teacher letting her friend take her skirt and top off, after she'd got soaked on the way to school, and dry off in front of the electric fire in his office.

"Well, she was wet through wasn't she? You have to get dry again or you get pneumonia."

She did not believe that one of her classmates was having an affair with their maths teacher. "He's just giving her extra tuition, isn't he?"

Even though her classmate's father had chased the teacher out of his house and down the hill.

She never believed babies were born quickly even though her daughter had arrived within ninety minutes of the first pain. "I slept through the rest, didn't I? I had a migraine."

The day before the world was due to end she announced: "Well, I don't know about the rest of you but I'm going shopping tomorrow."

When she turned up at the mall the next day, she was amazed to find all the shops shut and no lights on. There'd been no traffic on the way either. She mused that the power of disbelief was very strong but not particularly helpful.

WALKING

"You're sure you want to do this?" Tom was cramming what she had designated as essential into the large back-pack. A few more items, including a second backpack, were laid neatly on the bed.

"We have to, don't we? We can't pay the mortgage anymore."

"There ought to be a better way."

"There isn't though. Come, on. Better get on before the bailiffs arrive." Sal turned and looked out of the window. "Shall we mess up the garden as well? I'll get on with that if you like."

"Do you think you've got the strength?"

"I'm angry enough."

"Get to it, then, gal."

She picked up the think woolly jumper she'd chosen. It was going to fill the whole of one of the backpacks but it stood a chance of keeping her warm at night. "How long do you think we'll last out there?"

"You never know. It might make us stronger."

"And it might not."

"The trick is to keep walking, they say. Never stay too long in one place."

"I'll miss my nice comfortable bed."

"There'll be others. You'll see. That's why everybody always leaves the beds in one piece. So that they can be used by others. Come on, I've done here. Let's go and wreck the garden."

Sal nodded. She looked once more out of the window. A Walker was just passing. He looked about the same age as them. He held his back high and his face was tanned. There seemed to be a joy in his step. Sal waved. The Walker gave her a thumbs up. "Okay," she said to Tom. Let's get on with it. Quick as we can. And let's get out of here."

COMING AROUND AND GOING AROUND

So there's this woman. Spinster. Devoted daughter. Dies within a few days of her father. They're comfortably off. More than comfortably off, actually, but that wasn't always the case.

She worked for twenty years as a jobbing writer. She became quite good and even started advising new writers. She made enough money to get by and enjoyed it all anyway. A bit like me, really, and some of you.

Then she wrote the breakthrough novel. With that and the two that came after, she made a fortune. She invested in the railways and became seriously rich. So much so, that when one of the tenants whose house she'd mortgaged couldn't keep up with the repayments she told her solicitor to leave them in peace. You can afford to be generous, I guess, when you don't have to worry about money and work feels more like a hobby.

Now this novel: a lot of people say it was all about her, really. Maybe, maybe not, but she was, you know, writing what she knew, like they tell us to. And one of the main characters – the sister who is possibly the one most like her – skives off from her chores to read a book that the adults around her don't quite approve of. You'd never guess what it was. Only Charles Dickens' *Dombey and Son*.

Just goes to show, doesn't it? Same old, same old, coming around and going around, over and over. And both of them books still in print now.

Never say die, I say.

~~~~~~~~

Louisa May Alcott (1832 -1888) wrote *Little Women* in 1868. She was born in Germantown and died in Boston. She also wrote under the pen name A.M. Barnard.

JUST ADD WATER AND SUNSHINE

It was just about light and still a little cool for May. The ground was damp, but at least not sodden. Stella bent down and picked up a handful of soil. Yes, it was beautifully moist and soft. Today's job would be easy.

The van arrived before the neighbours set off. She'd called in a favour. Greg owed her for all the times she'd taken in the twins after school and then taken them home and put them to bed whilst he visited Karen in hospital.

They unloaded the trays of bedding plants and soon the front-lawn was filled with busy lizzies, lobelia, geraniums and other colourful plants she couldn't name.

"Good luck with it all," said Greg as he climbed back into the van. "Looks like you've got your work cut out. If you pull it off, though, it'll look great."

She worked all day, dibbing and planting, picking and choosing, bending and stretching. Her back ached, her fingers became black – she did have gloves but worked better without them and besides, she liked the feel of the soil in her hands – and the sun caught her face. She hardly stopped to eat or drink. Just as the commuters started returning she finished. She sat down on the patio bench and admired her work. *Instant garden,* she thought. *Just add water and sunshine.*

The phone rang. A couple wished to see the house. Could they come for a viewing in an hour's time?

She scrubbed her nails, showered and changed.

They were enthusiastic. "And the garden's so pretty," the young woman gushed.

Just as Rob's car pulled on to the drive, the phone rang again. It was the estate agent. The couple had made an offer on the house, spot on the asking price. After all those months and all those viewings.

She was glad she'd remembered her time in Holland when the instant gardens were delivered before breakfast in May.

THE PARTRIDGES AND THE PEAR TREES

Mary Patterson set out the dishes and spoons on the newly scrubbed table. Supper would be just salt and pepper soup, some of the stale bread Widow Sutton had given her and whatever the children brought back from their scavenging. There wouldn't be much. The autumn berries and fruits weren't yet ripe and the summer's were over. Albert might have trapped a bird if they were lucky – as long as Lord Brampton hadn't seen him.

It was getting late. Where were they?

The fire was ready for the cooking-pots and it was beginning to get dark. They'd been out a long time so they would be hungrier than ever. However much they'd brought would not be enough.

Maybe I should do as Lord Brampton asked, she thought. He had said that if she gave herself to him whenever the fancy took him he would see that she and her family would never starve. It was probably too late, now, anyway. After five children and another one on the way her looks had faded.

Albert had never objected. He'd said it was up to her. But she didn't want to do it and she suspected, or at least hoped, he was pleased.

Now, though, with the hunger months here again…

She heard them. Robbie was squealing with excitement, Trudy was singing, and Albert was whistling.

Peter ran in through the door, closely followed by Fran and Davey. "Ma, I got him with my catapult. Look what a big fat bird he is."

Mary gawped at the animal in his hands. "If Lord Brampton finds out…"

"He won't unless we tell him. Anyway, it was an accident, wasn't it Peter? You don't know what you're doing with that slinger." He ruffled his son's hair. "Not such a good shot as his old dad, though eh?" He pulled out two more partridges from behind his back and grinned.

"Oh, Albert," whispered Mary.

"And we found some windfalls on the ground," said Fran, handing her mother six wood-hard pears.

"They'll cook up all right, won't they love?" Albert slipped an arm around his wife's waist.

Mary nodded. The baby kicked so hard then that Albert felt it as well. They both laughed. The hunger months were on hold for a while yet and they'd scored twice against old Brampton.

"It's like Christmas come early," said Davey.

AN OBSESSION WITH NUMBERS

Clive Mortington-Jones loved numbers. As he stood waiting for the local commuter train on the first day back at work after the Christmas break, he worked out that his season ticket had actually gone up by 4.53%, a little unfair when his salary would go up by 1% at the end of the month, albeit backdated to August 2012, and when this morning's radio news had reported an average 4% rise on train fares. Who were the lucky bastards who were getting a below 4% increase that enabled the average increase to be 4%?

He counted the other people waiting. Ten on both sides of the track. So, absolutely spot on average. The week before Christmas it had fluctuated between 40% lower – perhaps reflecting the number of office parties and subsequent hangovers – and 30% higher – could that have been people taking the train into town for some last-minute shopping?

The 7.47 was running late. It was already 7.49. Expected 7.52 the board said. So, for 2013 100% late. If you calculated over the last twelve months, however it would be – he fished his notebook out of his inside jacket pocket and did a quick bit of mental arithmetic – 15.3%. Still not brilliant. It rather suggested fares ought to be reduced, not increased.

He started to work out what might be the effect of cutting fares. That would no doubt result in job losses, which would push up the percentage of people unemployed, which in turn would reduce the nation's spending power, further affecting the whole economy.

As the train approached the platform he reflected that yes, of course, it was obvious: fares had to rise.

He couldn't possibly know that Molly Andrews was one of the 5% of people who were glad to get back to work. It's likely that even if he hadn't have spent all of his time calculating, he wouldn't have noticed because she kept her face unreadable. The pretty but shy office junior had been missing her daily fix of staring at the good-looking young man who waited on the opposite platform for the 7.47 every day.

FLOODS RECEDING

"We're back where we started. They always do that with diversions."

"We don't need to go to the centre of the village. For god's sake, we've got a machine that can help us. Programme it to miss out Widdicombe."

Brett fiddles with the sat nav. It commands them to turn around if possible but as they start driving away from the road block it picks up their route and takes them behind the church and into open countryside.

The road is narrow. "I hope we don't meet anybody coming the other way," says Jenny clutching the sides of her seat.

There are the remains of fields on either side. They feel as if they are crossing a sea via a narrow causeway. Water laps at the sides of the road. They have to slow down for a couple with a dog. The dog-walkers stare at them for being audacious enough to come this way.

"Oh no. I can't look." Jenny shades her eyes. A dustcart is coming towards them.

Brett pulls into a passing place wondering whether there is a ditch between him and the flooded field. It would be a squeeze even in better conditions. Not being able to see, though, is scary.

The dustcart driver doesn't seem to care and rushes through, missing them by centimetres. Jenny breathes again. He drives on.

At one point the flood has crossed the road. "Careful," says Jenny, grabbing his arm.

The water is actually not all that deep. You can still see most of the hay bales, in the fields on either side. They're probably ruined. Even so Brett thinks of Noah and some sort of promise being made about there never being floods like that again. He would appreciate the Bible being right though as usual doubts it.

They come at last to a main road. It rises away from the flooded fields and Brett notices the muddy edges.

"See, it's okay," he says to Jenny. "The floods are receding."